# CONTENTS

D1081484

 **CALLING ALL TEACHERS!**

### ARE YOU DIPPY ABOUT DOLPHINS?

If you think you can make a big splash with a baby dolphin... Wildwatch wants to hear from you!

We're after a teacher (who needs to be a strong swimmer) to dive with bottlenose dolphins. Your job will be to watch a baby dolphin and keep a diary.

❏ *Enjoy the dips and dives of life with dolphins*

❏ *Action, adventure and drama guaranteed*

❏ *Excellent pay, plus expenses, including travel to Australia*

❏ *Enjoy the incredible scenery of Shark Bay*

❏ *Your diary will be published by Wildwatch!*

### DON'T DELAY – APPLY TODAY...

My name's Daisy Page and I'm having a really BAD day. I'm the librarian at Darkcliff School. At least I *was*. But this afternoon I walked out of school. Yes, I quit my job looking after the school library and

I'm not going back – not even if the head teacher licks the floor for me!

My friends call me Crazy Daisy because I'll have a go at anything – once. Karaoke singing, swimming in fancy dress, limbo dancing … I'm up for it and I've done it. Mind you, I haven't sung while swimming yet! Here's a photo of me singing karaoke…

This afternoon I had a go at the head teacher, Mr Smug-faced Smigley. He called me into his luxury office and said, "Daisy, I'm afraid certain savings have to be made in the library."

AND I'VE GOT A GREAT VOICE!

Mr Smigley has been giving me a tough time ever since he became head teacher. He told me off for wearing short skirts. He made me pay for the petrol in my car when I used it to go and buy books for the school. He won't let me have a lunch-time library helpers club, and… Well, I could go on and on. As soon as Mr Smigley said the word "savings" I felt my blood pressure shooting up like the marker on a test-your-strength machine at the fair.

There he sat in his grey suit, with his smug face, and his hands clasped on his expensive desk, while he told me I couldn't buy any more books for the children this year!

"Computers and the Internet – yes," he said. "But that's all. No books." And then he told me that my assistant and vital helper, Sue, would have to go.

DING! The test-your-strength marker hit the bell at the top. My blood was boiling…

"Over my dead body!" I snapped. "If Sue goes, I go!"

And I did…

When I got home I was still steaming with anger. With a big cross sigh, I picked up my newspaper and sat down to look at the job adverts. The Wildwatch advert was on the first page I looked at.

It was fate, I decided. I'm going to apply. I'm going to change my life and dive with dolphins! Well, that's if Wildwatch will let me! They don't call me Crazy Daisy for nothing! Look – I've already written the first day of my diary and I haven't even got the job yet!

# MAMA MIA – IT'S MONKEY MIA!

### July 2

Here I am sitting under a tree in Western Australia, all set to go dolphin watching – but there's not a dolphin in sight. Mind you, there isn't much of anything except red earth and a dusty black crow perching sleepily on a telegraph pole. Oh yes, and some noisy parrots flitting and squawking amongst the spiky trees.

This map will show you where I am...

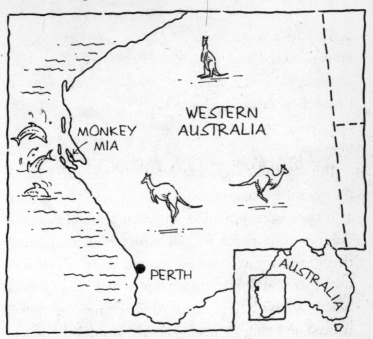

I'd better explain what's going on! Yes, you've guessed it – I got the Wildwatch job!

I told the lady who interviewed me that I was a librarian and not a teacher.

"It doesn't matter," she smiled. "As long as you can write a diary for children."

"I can definitely do that," I replied and I added that I'm also a strong swimmer.

It's true. When I was younger I won cups for swimming. I'm sure that's how I got my big freckly shoulders! And I'm crazy about dolphins...

When I was small my sister Poppy (yes, our mum had a thing about flowers) and I had loads of pets. We had a cat, a hamster, a rabbit and a dog. And we loved to help care for them.

ME AGED 8

But dolphins were my favourite animals. I loved the way the shape of their mouths made them look as if they were smiling. And when I found out that dolphins can make friends with children, I loved them even more! I always wanted to have my very own special dolphin friend to play with. No wonder when Wildwatch phoned to offer me the job I danced and sang "I'm so excited!" around the room. I felt over the moon!

The plan is that I'll be staying at Monkey Mia. It's one of the few places where you can get really close to wild dolphins. I'll be spending half the week going out in a boat with a local dolphin expert named Sam Williams. And when Sam's writing up his dolphin research, I'll be on the beach writing my diary. And hopefully watching dolphins from the land!

I arrived in Australia two days ago and I stayed in a hotel in Perth while I got over my jet lag. This morning Sam's pal, a guy named Eric, picked me up and drove me to the Overlander Roadhouse. Then Eric drove off with a cheery wave and a big cloud of red dust. And that's how I came to be sitting under this tree waiting for Sam to turn up and take me to Monkey Mia.

But where is Sam?

## Two hours later

Yes, where *is* Sam?

Now there's one thing you need to know about me, especially if you're going to read my diary, and that is I don't like waiting. My ideal day is spent charging about, even if I am chasing my tail half the time…

But today, instead of getting too bothered, I wrote these notes. I'm sure you'll find them handy once I get to see some dolphins!

# DAISY'S DOLPHIN NOTES
## BOTTLENOSE BASICS

1. There's actually about 35 dolphin species (spee-shes) or types. Scientists aren't too sure whether bottlenose dolphins are one species or several that look very similar.

2. Bottlenose dolphins are so-called because their snouts look like old-fashioned bottles.

**The Monkey Mia dolphins belong to a type that lives in the Pacific and Indian Oceans.**

**3. Here's what a bottlenose dolphin looks like...**

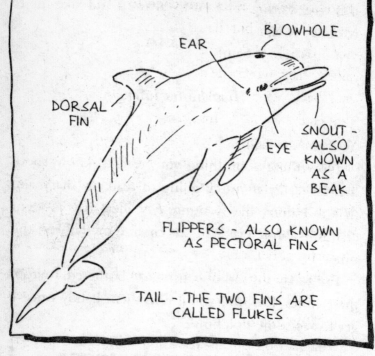

BLOWHOLE

EAR

DORSAL FIN

SNOUT - ALSO KNOWN AS A BEAK

EYE

FLIPPERS - ALSO KNOWN AS PECTORAL FINS

TAIL - THE TWO FINS ARE CALLED FLUKES

As I waited for Sam, I found myself daydreaming. Sam, I decided, was going to be the tall, dark, handsome type. He would look like a film star and own a big white yacht with a giant-sized cold drinks cabinet. He'd pour me a drink while I decided whether to lie in the sun or perhaps play in the water with my special baby dolphin. OK, so it was a lovely daydream while it lasted.

As soon as Sam appeared, the dream vanished quicker than the black smelly smoke spluttering from the back of his rusty old car. The gears made a nasty grinding sound as he screeched to a halt.

Sam *is* tall, but he's not dark. He's got silvery hair, which he'd tied back with an old shoelace, and his scraggy beard looks like it has grown without its owner noticing. His face is almost as red as the soil and he was sweating rather a lot.

"Debbie!" he cried, grabbing my hand. "I'm sorry! There's something up with the gearbox. But it's fixed now. Well, sort of…"

Sam had oil on his arms and a little smudge was smeared on the end of his nose.

"Daisy!" I corrected.

Sam didn't drive me to Monkey Mia. He was worried that the gearbox wouldn't stand the trip there and then on to Denham where he lives. So instead we drove straight to Denham. And Sam was right – by the time we reached the village, there was only one gear that wanted to work.

At the back of Sam's battered bungalow is a veranda that looks out over the wide blue Shark Bay. And that's where we sat to talk over our dolphin-watching plans and enjoy the sunset. Sam's interested in how dolphins live in groups and the sounds they make to keep in touch. When he's not watching dolphins he's usually at home trying to sort out his untidy piles of notes, or writing dolphin articles for magazines. Sometimes he's repairing his boat.

"I've got a confession," said Sam. "I'm having a bit of trouble with the old boat at present. It could be a few days before we're out on the water."

"OK," I replied, taking a deep breath. Nothing was going right today.

But in front of me, as the sun slid slowly into the bay, the water turned a shiny golden colour and I could almost hear the sizzle as it hit the sea. It was so beautiful that I stopped feeling annoyed about the broken-down boat. Instead I smiled and turned to Sam.

"I'm going to like it here," I said.

## July 3

I spent the night at a motel in Denham and took a taxi to Monkey Mia in the morning. Sam did offer me a bed in his spare room but something he said about hoping I didn't mind cockroaches put me off.

Monkey Mia isn't what I expected. Even the name is different! I've been calling it "Monkey Mee-a" when it should be "Monkey My-a". I imagined it as an empty beach millions of miles from anywhere. Well, that's how it looks on a map. Instead I found myself in a tourist resort. Here's a map of the area…

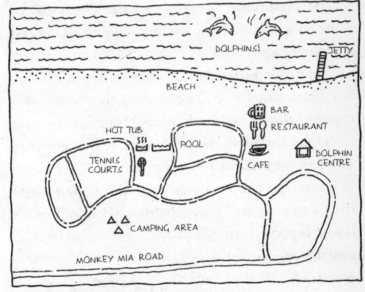

There's a big wooden dolphin information centre with a sign telling visitors how to treat dolphins. And there's a café and a restaurant, a shop, swimming pool, tennis courts and barbecue areas. There are tents and mobile homes and villas and people. They've even planted palm trees and a gorgeous green lawn. And don't get me wrong, it's lovely for visitors – but it's not exactly a wilderness.

I actually said this to Clyde, the young man who showed me to my caravan.

"Monkey Mia used to be a lot smaller," he said. "But when people heard about the dolphins they started turning up in their thousands. And they all needed a place to stay."

This afternoon I went for a wander. The thing you really notice round here, well the thing that I noticed, are the colours.

There's the dusty red earth, the sparkling blue sea and the almost-as-blue sky. The dusty bushes bloom with colourful flowers and the beach is a bright sandy white.

At the southern end of the bay is a place where dugongs (also known as sea cows) live. They're big brainless seal-like creatures that spend their whole lives lazing in the water. In the olden days sailors were supposed to mistake dugongs for mermaids. Well, I saw a dugong today and it had a split lip and a hairy face. I can't quite imagine a sailor falling in love with it!

NOT A BEAUTY!

Oh well, that's enough writing for today. I'm off to chill out on the beach with a long cold lemonade.

And tomorrow … tomorrow, hopefully, I'll get my first glimpse of the dolphins. Here's hoping!

## *July 4*

This morning I woke up feeling really excited. It was only about 5 am, but I'm still a bit jet-lagged and luckily I'm an early riser, so I decided to look at my notes from the training day I went on at Wildwatch. If I was going to meet dolphins today, I wanted to know what to do…

# DEALING WITH DOLPHINS

1. Don't touch a dolphin unless a dolphin touches you.

2. Never touch a dolphin's blowhole. Imagine a giant trying to pick your nose with its big grubby finger and you'll know why dolphins don't like this.

PICK, PICK

3. If you do touch a dolphin, touch its sides. Dolphin skin is sensitive and they're easily injured, so be gentle.

4. Try not to sneeze over a dolphin - they can catch colds from us.

5. If a dolphin offers you a fish, take it politely and never try to give it back. Don't worry - you don't have to eat the fish!

I felt sleepy after my early start and I was soon nodding off in the warm morning sunshine. I would have missed the dolphin feeding if I hadn't heard a boy shout: "Here come the dolphins!"

All at once, everyone on the beach dashed towards the boy. Mums and kids chattered with excitement and I saw white-haired old couples stepping carefully hand in hand over the sand. Most of the visitors were eagerly clutching cameras.

A ranger in green waterproof trousers was standing in the water holding a bucket of fish. She was ordering the crowd to keep back. And there in the sparkling shallows lay the dolphins. They rolled onto their sides like cats, and the sunshine glistened on their shiny grey bodies.

The dolphins were looking at the ranger with their big smiling mouths wide open. "Feed us!" they seemed to be pleading – although their fast clicking calls sounded more like whizzing whirring bicycle wheels.

Everyone was nudging and pushing forward to peer at the dolphins. I could hear excited murmurs and whispers of "Aren't they beautiful!"

The ranger had chosen a little boy to carry the fish bucket and a girl to feed the dolphins. Carefully and slowly the girl knelt down in the warm, clear water and offered a fish to each dolphin. The dolphins politely took the fish from the girl's hand. They didn't snatch like some animals would. They gently took the silver floppy fish in their jaws just like you or me accepting a teacake, then they gulped it down. The crowd began to clap and the girl gazed at the dolphins with big shining eyes.

With each fish, the ranger moved the girl a little further along the beach and the dolphins followed them. That way, everyone got a good view. And each time I heard a buzz of chatter and more cameras clicking and whirring.

As for me, I was spellbound. In fact I was so busy watching the dolphins feeding that I nearly forgot to take this picture.

FEEDING THE DOLPHINS

After the feeding was over, the dolphins swam away. And I had a chance to chat with Cheryl, the ranger. I'll talk to anyone and everyone is happy to

CHERYL

talk to me. Maybe it's because I've got a friendly face? Anyway, Cheryl and I got talking and we ended up sipping cappuccino coffees in the cafe.

"The dolphins get local fish," said Cheryl, "but not too many. We don't want them to depend on us and forget how to hunt. The funny thing is that the dolphins don't have to come at all. There are plenty of fish in the bay."

"Really?" I said in surprise, wiping a frothy cappuccino moustache from my upper lip.

"Really!" smiled Cheryl. "Sometimes they aren't even hungry. They just play with the fish, like kids who don't want to eat."

I tried to imagine what it's like to be one of those dolphins. You drag yourself onto a beach, something no dolphin would do normally. You risk sunburn and being hurt by those strange pink chattering creatures with their funny wriggly flippers. But you still do it. Why? Well, if the dolphins aren't always after the fish, maybe they actually like seeing us…

# July 5

The dolphins came again this morning but I wasn't chosen to feed them. I didn't even get to carry the smelly old fish bucket! Cheryl told me yesterday that she usually asks children to feed the dolphins.

"For some reason," said Cheryl, "the dolphins are fond of children. And of course the children love the dolphins."

Watching the dolphins today gave me an idea for a little experiment. I wanted to know how it feels to be a dolphin being fed. Hey, maybe you'd like to try it too?

## DAISY'S DOLPHIN NOTES
### HOW TO BEG LIKE A DOLPHIN

1. Lie down on your tummy in some shallow water. If you aren't on the beach, you could lie on the floor.
2. Now look upwards and lift your upper body on your flippers. (If you don't have any flippers, you could try propping yourself up on your elbows.)

**3. Open your mouth as wide as you can and make a squeaky eheheheheheh! sound. Guess what? You're begging for fish just like a dolphin. Let's hope someone doesn't shove a slimy great fish in your mouth!**

I bet you felt a bit uncomfortable lying on your tummy and looking up at everyone! And I'm sure the dolphins don't feel too comfy either.

## July 6

I opened my eyes to find myself lying in a grassy field. Except that I wasn't on the ground. Somehow I was floating in mid-air! I was all alone and the field was quiet. Above me stretched a big blue empty sky.

I spread my arms and wriggled my body and began to fly. I glided fast and silently through the clear air. Except that it wasn't air – it was water! And instead of arms and legs I had flippers and a funny finny tail. I had turned into a dolphin!

At that moment I guessed something you've probably guessed already. This wasn't really happening. *I was dreaming!* But that didn't bother me. I felt peaceful and happy as I whooshed over the thick green grass – which was actually seagrass, a type of seaweed that grows in Shark Bay.

Beneath me, I could see little gravelly stones and creeping crabs and shiny silvery fish and scuttling shrimps. I felt hungry. I wanted to nose down and feed on a fish or grab a crab or scrunch a shrimp with my small pointy teeth.

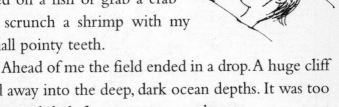

YUM YUM!

Ahead of me the field ended in a drop. A huge cliff fell away into the deep, dark ocean depths. It was too deep and dark for me to see much.

OH NO! I thought, I'm going to fall! But then I remembered that I was a dolphin and I wasn't afraid.

I swooped over the cliff with a great laugh bubbling up inside me. Just then a big blast of cold water blew up like an icy gust of air. And that's when I woke up with a chilly breeze on my face from the open caravan window.

Wow! I thought, as I lay on my hard lumpy bed. That was some dream!

The dream inspired me to find out more about where dolphins lived.

# DAISY'S DOLPHIN NOTES
## DOLPHIN HOMES

1. Bottlenose dolphins live in all the world's seas except the icy cold oceans at the ends of the Earth. That gives the dolphins a very big home indeed since oceans cover nearly 71% of our planet.

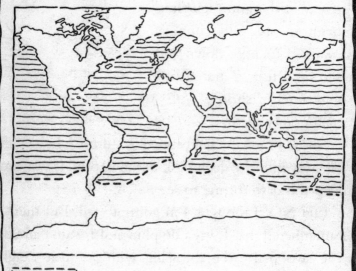

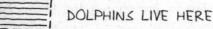
DOLPHINS LIVE HERE

2. Bottlenose dolphins in colder seas often grow bigger than those who live in the warmer areas. Round Monkey Mia they're about 2 metres long but off the chilly coasts of North America they can grow to 3.5 metres.

**3. The big cliff in my dream is called the continental shelf and it's where the sea bed drops away from the level of the seashore to the really deep ocean. Lots of fish live in this area and so do dolphins because they follow the fish.**

## July 7

I've been waiting for a message from Sam about the boat. But so far not a whisper. I was getting tired of waiting, so today I rang him up.

Sam didn't sound too happy. "The engine's gone!" he complained. "I'm having to send to Perth for a replacement part. It's probably going to be another few days before everything's fixed. I was meaning to ring…"

So here I am stuck on dry land like a dolphin out of water. Don't get me wrong, I do like it here. And yet I want to get closer to dolphins than just watching them being fed. And I'm feeling a bit guilty. I've been here one whole week and I still haven't chosen a dolphin to write this diary about…

## July 8

Do you believe in fate? Do you believe that wishes can come true? After this morning I think I do!

You know how yesterday I was complaining about not finding a dolphin? Well, this morning I found him! Or maybe he found me?

For the last couple of days I've been getting up at about 4 am and going for a walk. I love these dawn strolls when the air is cool and there's no one else about.

So there I was, taking a rest on the jetty. That's the wooden walkway that sticks into the sea near the dolphin information centre. The water gurgled against the wooden posts supporting the jetty and made swirly patterns of light and bubbles. I gazed down into the water... And there he was! Had he been there all the time? Had he come so quietly that I hadn't noticed? I couldn't say. All I knew was that he was there. A baby dolphin in the dawn with little waves washing over his grey sides. It was so quiet I could even hear the dolphin's breathing – phoohoof, phoohoof...

MY BABY DOLPHIN

Then I saw his mother. The mother dolphin had already seen me but she hadn't swum away. She just lay there quietly in the water watching me with friendly interest. I knew I had to get closer.

"Don't go away. I'm coming," I whispered to the dolphins. "I'm coming."

With a beating heart, I quietly got to my feet and crept back along the jetty to the beach. It was a chilly morning, but I didn't care! I waded into the water. It was so cold it stung my skin and took my breath away, but my eyes never left the dolphins…

Deeper and deeper I waded until the cold water was licking around my shuddering tummy. And just then the mother dolphin rolled and my finger brushed her side.

Her warm skin felt soft and smooth like wet velvet. Little electric tingles zipped along my fingertips and all the way up my back. They took my breath away. Now I was close I got a sense of how big and strong the mother dolphin was. If she stood on her tail next to me she'd be half a metre taller. But she was gentle too. I looked into her eyes and I didn't want to look away.

YOU'RE TALL!

1.5m

2m

I found myself talking to her.

"Hi!" I whispered. "My name's Daisy. I've come a long way to see you. You're so beautiful! Is that your baby? He's lovely. What's he called?"

I was so excited, I was gabbling a bit. But the dolphins didn't mind. They buzzed and whirred and squeaked in reply. The mother dolphin dipped her head in the water and let out a bubble of air. It gave me an idea.

"I'll call you Bubble!" I said.

Just as I was saying those words the baby dolphin who had been swimming in a circle came back. He rubbed his mum with his pointy snout and let out a little squeak as if to say, "Hi, mum, I'm back. What's up?"

"And I'll call you Squeak," I told the baby.

BUBBLE AND SQUEAK

Squeak turned away into the deeper water, all the time chattering to his mum. Then a few moments later, with a single smooth flick of her tail, she glided away and vanished like a ghost in the misty dawn.

I staggered out of the sea. I was shivering with cold and shaking with excitement. The chilly water dripped off my soaking trousers and squelched in my soggy shoes. But I didn't care. As I dripped my way back to the caravan I said to myself, "They've chosen me. And I've found the baby dolphin I'm going to write about. I'm going to tell the story of Bubble and Squeak!"

And I felt so happy I hugged myself and sang "I could be so lucky!"

In my mind's eye I could still see the dolphins. Bubble's dorsal fin was slightly bent to the left. I felt sure I'd know her next time. And I knew I'd see her and Squeak again...

## July 10

I've just spoken to Sam and the engine's fixed! Tomorrow, at last, we're going dolphin watching! It's quite late, but I've just been for a walk along the beach. The big round moon hung low over the water, the white sand gleamed like old bones, and the water was a shiny inky black. But the bay wasn't quiet.

I could just make out little splashes and pattering sounds, which I guessed were fish leaping from the water. Then I heard the dolphins. Phoohoof! Phoohoof! they snorted as they came up for air and dived once more. I guessed they were after the fish and I wondered if one of them was Bubble. Perhaps she was hunting a silvery fish for her supper. The thought of dolphins reminded me of tomorrow and my heart leapt up in a little tapdance of excitement.

TAPPITY-TAP

Yes, I'll be sailing in Sam's boat and with luck my dream will come true – I'll be diving with dolphins. I just can't wait for tomorrow!

I just … can't … wait!

# BUBBLE AND SQUEAK

## *July 11*

I was ready and waiting on the jetty when Sam's boat, *Cindy*, chugged out of the morning mist

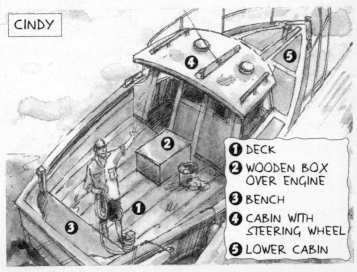

CINDY

1 DECK
2 WOODEN BOX OVER ENGINE
3 BENCH
4 CABIN WITH STEERING WHEEL
5 LOWER CABIN

So much for the white yacht in my daydream! Sam's boat turned out to be a weather-beaten relic of a bygone age. (A bit like its owner, me-thinks!)

"Climb aboard!" yelled Sam above the cough and splutter of the newly mended engine.

Sam helped me load my things into the boat. I didn't have that much – at least I didn't think so!

THINGS TO TAKE DOLPHIN WATCHING
1. Snorkel and mask. Vital for diving with dolphins if we can find them!
2. Swimming costume and towel – even more vital!
3. Diary and pencil
4. Binoculars
5. Waterproof camera and lots of spare film
6. Seasickness pills
7. Warm clothes and waterproof jacket (it can be chilly on the water)
8. Brush and comb, sunglasses, sunscreen and sun hat
9. Sandwiches and lots of water to drink

SEASICK PILLS

SUNSCREEN

Before I tell you about the day, I've got some exciting news! Sam knows Bubble and Squeak! He's even got photos of them!

"Hmm … I know they're in here somewhere," murmured Sam as he flicked through the well-thumbed pages of his big battered photo album.

The pages of Sam's album were packed with dolphin pictures. There were speeding dolphins and feeding dolphins, leaping dolphins and sleeping dolphins. Some photos showed the whole dolphin, but most of them were just dorsal fins.

"That's generally all you need to tell them apart," said Sam. And he pointed out dolphins with ragged fins and fins with holes and odd patterns of scars.

BASHED-UP DOLPHIN

"Ah-ha, here she is! Bubble, as you call her, is a female. She's about 15 or 16 years old and I think Squeak's her second calf." (A calf is the proper name for a baby dolphin.)

"So Squeak's got a brother or sister?!" I said excitedly.

"Yes, a sister," said Sam. "Here she is…" Sam showed me a photo of a dolphin that looked like a smaller version of Bubble, complete with the same bent-over fin.

This is so-o-o amazing! First I meet the mum and baby. Now I find out the baby has a sister! But where are they all?

"You've got to be patient," said Sam. "Sometimes you can hang around all day and they don't show. All we can do is head for the places where I've seen them in the past and hope we're lucky."

## Later

Patience isn't a Daisy virtue, I decided, as I fidgeted my numb backside on the hard wooden bench. I could just see Monkey Mia in the distance and the thin red line of the cliffs that lined the shore. But apart from that, there was nothing else to see.

The water was as smooth as glass and reflected the clear blue sky like a mirror. As the mist lifted and the sun rose higher, it grew hotter and the bright sun made dancing patterns on the still water.

I smeared sunscreen on my face until I looked like a native American in war paint. And I waited ... and chatted to Sam about swimming with dolphins.

"Before you get in the water with dolphins," said Sam, "the most important thing is that you need to be sure they are dolphins ... and not sharks."

"Sharks?!" I gulped. I remembered something about sharks from my Wildwatch course.

Sam chuckled. "Tiger sharks swim in these waters. Why do you think it's called Shark Bay? But it's easy to tell them apart from dolphins – their fins are less rounded and they don't rise and fall during swimming, they just sort of cut through the water. And dolphins breathe air, so you can hear them coming up to breathe."

SINISTER SHARK

DIPPY DOLPHIN

I wasn't sure if that made me feel better about getting in the water.

"Don't look so worried," said Sam calmly. "I'll be your look-out and if I see one I'll yell 'SHARK!' We should be OK, sharks aren't too common at this time of year and they mostly appear at dusk."

Er, thanks, Sam.

I decided that it would take more than hungry sharks to put me off diving with dolphins. After all I'm diving after a dream. And I was just thinking about my dream when the dolphins appeared.

It all happened quicker than I can write...

"Dolphins! Here they come!" shouted Sam.

I didn't have time to worry about sharks. I dashed into the cabin to change and soon I was wriggling into my fins, fiddling with my mask and wondering where I'd left my snorkel tube.

WRIGGLE, WRIGGLE

FLAP, FLAP

"Hurry up!" called Sam. "They might not hang around!"

I'm a good swimmer but diving isn't my strong point, and there was no time for a graceful dive. I shuffled across the deck, feeling like a clown in my big floppy fins, and plopped into the water. All at once my head was under a greeny-blue wave and all I could see was bubbles.

I spluttered into the air as a dolphin rose out of the waves and arched down in front of me. I took a deep breath and decided to duck my head under the water. It was like looking though a murky blue fog.

But the water wasn't deep and I could see the waving seagrass on the sandy bottom.

Dolphins dashed out of the foggy water faster than torpedoes. For a second I thought one would crash into me but it swerved aside. I splashed gasping into the air. I opened my mouth and promptly swallowed a pint of sick-making salty seawater. Gagging and burping I looked for the boat.

Sam was leaning over the side. "How many can you see?" he called.

"I dunno!" I shouted back, and dipped my head under the water again.

The dolphins were circling, I could see shadowy shapes all around me. I could hear them squeaking and clicking. I longed to dive down after them but my body felt too heavy and clumsy. Compared with the fast, graceful dolphins I felt like an elephant in a ballet class.

It was such a funny thought that I felt a giant giggling fit bubbling up inside me. As I stuck my head out of the water, I broke into a big hearty laugh.

"Are you OK?" asked Sam.

"Yes!" I shrieked. "I'm just so-o-o happy!"

By the time I'd stopped laughing, the dolphins had gone. And the bay was as calm and quiet as if they'd never been there.

The dolphins didn't come back and after another very long wait, we chugged slowly back to Monkey Mia where Sam dropped me off at the jetty. After a day on the water, my skin felt dry and wrinkly and my legs had turned to jelly. Thanks to the hot sun and the sea, my skin was red and salty. But my heart was still bumping and thumping with the thrill of diving with the dolphins. All I could think of was seeing them again.

WOBBLE
WOBBLE

## July 12

I set off this morning in a state of high excitement. Would I be lucky enough to swim with the dolphins again? As before, we waited ages for the action. Yes, dolphin watching can feel more like dolphin WAITING. And dolphin waiting can feel like forever!

Today I took my dolphin books and wrote a story about Squeak's early days.

# Squeak's story

Squeak was born on Christmas Day. For twelve months he'd been snuggling up inside his mum's warm tummy. And, just like that, out he plopped, tail first, into the big chilly ocean. Brrr! The cold really took his breath away. And it could have been fatal since he didn't know how to breathe!

But Squeak's mum helped him to swim upwards and he found himself gasping in the air. At first he wasn't too good at holding his breath but he sensed that he would have to learn fast.

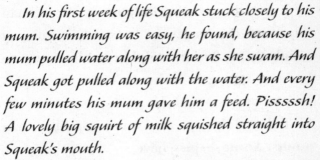

In his first week of life Squeak stuck closely to his mum. Swimming was easy, he found, because his mum pulled water along with her as she swam. And Squeak got pulled along with the water. And every few minutes his mum gave him a feed. Pisssssh! A lovely big squirt of milk squished straight into Squeak's mouth.

Every day Squeak felt a little stronger and braver. After the first week his mum left him in the care of his dolphin granny and went *off to catch fish. But one day Squeak thought it would be fun to go off and catch fish like his mum. His mum didn't like it. She fetched him back and walloped him with her big finny tail.*

Sam laughed when I read him Squeak's story.

"I'm not sure Squeak was born on Christmas Day," he chuckled. "I guess it was sometime around then, but I wasn't around to see it."

Sam told me some more really vital things you need to know about dolphin babies.

# DAISY'S DOLPHIN NOTES
## DOLPHIN BABIES

1. A new-born baby dolphin is more than one-third the length of its mother and can weigh up to 20 kg. Dolphin babies must be big and strong in order to swim as soon as they're born.

2. Baby dolphins are more chubby than adults. Some babies have whiskers, which they lose as they grow up. Just imagine if human babies had big bushy moustaches!

GOO GOO!

3. Dolphin milk is many times richer than human milk. It's full of the fat and protein that a dolphin baby needs to grow quickly.

4. A dolphin mum needs to be a good hunter to catch enough fish to make milk. But sometimes her sisters can help to look after the baby. The baby starts to eat fish after about four months but it continues to drink milk for another two years or more.

"And now," said Sam, "you ought to add a bit more to your story. Something about Squeak growing up."

When Sam's explaining something he's got this habit of blinking fast and polishing his glasses. He reminds me of a teacher.

"I'm all ears," I said.

"Well, when Squeak's about three, he'll join a sub-adult group…"

Er, time for a quick translation, readers.

Do you like going to school? If you said "NO", you might like to join a dolphin sub-adult group! It's like a school with no teachers (not even any librarians) and children make the rules. Does that sound good? You can play with your friends or visit your mum when you feel like it! But no one tells you what to do! Does that sound fun? Yes, I thought you'd say that!

According to Sam, boy and girl dolphins have their own groups but some of the girl dolphins like to play with the boys. I thought back to when I was a girl. All the boys were in gangs and the girls didn't like playing with them. But I was different. I loved climbing trees and playing football with the boys. In fact I was one of the lads! I smiled at the memory and gazed at the empty sea. Still no dolphins, I thought with a sigh.

And today the dolphins didn't show up at all.

## *July 13*

After yesterday's disappointment I wasn't getting my hopes up, but I spent the morning glued to my binoculars just in case. After a while I began to imagine there was a dolphin hiding behind every wave.

HEE HEE! SHE CAN'T SEE ME!

Sam steered *Cindy* to a sheltered part of the shore so that I could have a swim before lunch. And that's how I came to be in the water at just the right time…

I was floating on my back, gazing up at a wispy cloud. My arms and legs were spread wide. Suddenly there were two dolphins close by. And incredibly, amazingly, they were … Bubble and Squeak!

I knew them at once and I was sure they knew me too. Suddenly Bubble was gliding around me making friendly buzzing, squeaking sounds. Squeak was exploring the shallow water a few metres away. As I watched, he rolled in the water and dived under his mum, tickling her tummy with his flipper.

Just like last time, I found myself chattering away to the dolphins…

"Hi, it's me, Daisy, remember? It's great to see you!"

Well, that's what I was trying to say, but since I had the snorkel tube stuck in my mouth and I was standing in water nearly as deep as me, it came out like…

BA, ISH BE, HAGY…

And the rest made even less sense.

To see Bubble and Squeak swim is the most incredible thing ever! "Swim" isn't the right word — they seem to slice through water like a kite cuts through the air. They looked so lovely that my eyes filled with tears of joy and my nose began to run.

I don't know how long I watched the dolphins splash and roll and glide and nudge one another.

I just know that it wasn't long enough. Then, without warning, the dolphins turned and headed into deeper water as if answering some secret call.

## July 17

I've had four days on land while Sam catches up on his work, so I've spent the time food shopping and watching the daily dolphin feeding from the beach.

The most exciting day was yesterday when Bubble turned up to be fed! I wasn't totally surprised to see her. Sam said that Gabby, the old dolphin, who almost always turns up for free fish, is Bubble's mum. And Bubble sometimes comes with her.

GRANNY GABBY

Anyway, yesterday Bubble showed up with Squeak close by. I felt madly jealous of the little boy who got to feed Bubble with a small shiny fish!

"It should have been me!" I muttered darkly to myself. I'd have given a small fortune for the honour, I really would!

Squeak wouldn't come to be fed. He circled in the deeper water calling to his mum. Of course, the tourists were thrilled to see him.

"Oh look, it's a baby!" they exclaimed.

"Come closer!" pleaded a little girl from the water's edge.

But Squeak kept away. I expect he was scared by the attention and he just wanted to go off somewhere quiet with his mum.

## July 18

It's great to be back on the water again – even if Sam's not letting me swim!

"I'd like to try a focal follow this week," he told me.

"Follow what?" I asked, feeling like a dolphin dimwit.

"Focal follow," said Sam. "It means choosing just one dolphin and following it about all day. You get to find out how a dolphin spends its time, who its dolphin friends are and so on. But there won't be any chance to swim, I'm afraid."

"OK," I said. "You're the captain."

Of course, I was secretly hoping that we'd do our focal follow on Bubble! And today was my lucky day, as you're about to find out!

*Cindy* was in clear shallow water not far out from Monkey Mia. Suddenly the boat wobbled slightly as Bubble rose in the water beside us. She tilted her head to one side with friendly interest.

"Hi!" she seemed to say. "Come for a swim – the water's lovely!"

FANCY A SWIM?

"I can't!" I said. "I've got to stay on the boat."

Yes, I was so sure the dolphin was talking to me, I actually answered back!

Sam gave me a funny look. "Looks like we've found our dolphin to follow," he said.

Then Squeak bobbed up in the water like a cork. He took a deep breath and dived once more. Bubble plunged after him. I gazed down into the clear water. I could see the dolphins rubbing and stretching their snouts to tickle each other under their flippers. It was like watching an underwater dance.

A moment later Bubble came up to breathe. She gave me a quick naughty look and suddenly her blowhole opened and she sprayed me with fishy salty sea spray. Phoof pissssssh! It went straight in my face! I think it was Bubble's idea of a joke.

Sam was hit too. He was kneeling beside me recording what the dolphins were up to on his tape recorder. It's how Sam makes notes for his research. He says the dolphins move too fast for him to write things down. I was very impressed – Sam kept talking and didn't even stop to wipe the spray off his glasses!

Meanwhile Squeak was still underwater. I could just see him nosing amongst the wavy seagrass in search of small darting fish. But he was doing it in a slow, half-hearted way like a bored little boy at a loss for something to do.

All at once there was lots for Sam to talk about. Without warning, Squeak shot upwards. But he didn't stop. He leapt clean out of the water as if it was a really hot bath.

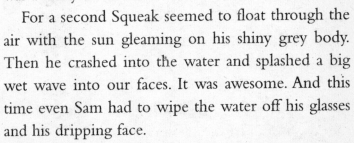

EEK! IT'S HOT!

For a second Squeak seemed to float through the air with the sun gleaming on his shiny grey body. Then he crashed into the water and splashed a big wet wave into our faces. It was awesome. And this time even Sam had to wipe the water off his glasses and his dripping face.

Squeak was showing off. Two other dolphins had shown up. They were another mum and her baby.

And all the dolphins seemed to know each other. The two mother dolphins rolled their bellies in greeting. And the two babies rushed off like a pair of mini guided missiles. In a splash of a tail they were chasing and butting like playful puppies. Except, of course, you won't find puppies playing underwater!

Meanwhile the dolphin mums were resting quietly side by side. But just then Squeak's friend nipped his mum's tummy and she gave him a cross whack with her flipper. And that gave me an idea for their names.

"I'll call you Slap," I said to the mother dolphin. "And you," I told her naughty baby, "you will be called Nipper."

But, of course, the dolphins weren't listening.

Slap and Bubble went back to their doze in the warm sunshine and Squeak and Nipper began to play a game called "I can leap higher than you".

Again and again they flew out of the water.

I could almost hear Squeak yelling, "Watch me! I can jump into space if I want to!"

And Nipper shouting back, "Yeah, but I can jump higher than space!"

And so it went on for a couple of hours and I loved every leap and splash of it! Although this was meant to be a focal follow, we didn't do much following of Bubble since she stayed where she was for much of the day.

Eventually, as the evening sky was lit by a splendid sunset, we chugged happily home.

LEAPING BABIES

# July 19

Today was windy. The green waves smacked against *Cindy*'s sides and tried to spin her around and tip her up and down. I was really glad I had my seasickness pills!

At lunchtime, I staggered into the shelter of the cabin and asked Sam about something that had been bothering me since last week.

"You know there are sharks in the bay?" I began.

"Mmm," replied Sam, who was peering at his map and trying to work out where the dolphins could be.

"Well, how much danger are they to dolphins?"

Sam folded his map and stuffed it in the pocket of his baggy old jacket.

"Sharks like to eat dolphins when they can – but other creatures can be dangerous to dolphins as well."

And off he went in full-blown teacher mode, telling me all the deadly details. It was scary stuff, so I hope you're feeling brave…

## DAISY'S DOLPHIN NOTES
### FOUR FATAL FISH AND A KILLER WHALE

1. Tiger sharks often attack dolphins after dark. They target baby dolphins or old, sick dolphins.

I'M HUNGRY!

2. The spines of a scorpion fish are tipped with a deadly poison that can melt flesh and kill a dolphin.

3. Stonefish hide in rocks and look – surprise, surprise – like stones. The poison from their spines is said to cause the worst pain in the world.

4. Stingrays use their sharp tails like whips. The tails can wound a dolphin.

5. Dolphins can be eaten by orcas (also known as killer whales). Orcas are sometimes seen in Shark Bay.

As Sam was talking, little bells started to ring between my ears.

"I know all this!" I broke in. "They warned me about these fish on my Wildwatch course."

"That's not surprising," said Sam glumly. "These fish can harm humans too. But young dolphins are in worse danger because they don't know which fish are dangerous. I guess that's one reason why so many young dolphins die."

"Die?" I asked. "How many?"

Sam shook his head and sighed. "As many as half could die before they're two years old."

"That's terrible!" I burst out. "But it won't happen to Squeak, not if I can help him!"

"Yes, hopefully nothing will happen at all," smiled Sam. "But the world is a dangerous place for a baby dolphin."

I tried not to think of Squeak with a poisoned spine stuck in his poor little body.

"No, of course it won't!" I said shaking my head.

But as the day wore on without a sight of the dolphins, I did begin to wonder … had something *already* happened?

# THE DIPPY DOLPHIN SOAP SHOW

## *July 20*

With a lovely long sigh of relief, I spotted Bubble and Squeak. They were roughly where they were the day before yesterday and as far as I could tell they looked fine! This time, though, they didn't stay long. They just hung around long enough to circle the boat and smile up at us from the water.

And then they were off and we lost them in the shallow water of a big seagrass bed. But for once I wasn't too disappointed. I had this strange idea that they'd just shown up to tell me they were fine.

DON'T WORRY, DAISY!

# July 25

Today Bubble and Squeak weren't on their own. Leaning over *Cindy*'s side, I could see dark dolphin shapes in the water. And as I watched, the dolphins came up for quick phoohoofs of air.

At first I wasn't sure what was going on.

"Who are the other dolphins?" I asked.

"They look like Bubble's family," said Sam, who had been talking excitedly into his tape recorder. "Look, there's Gabby – Bubble's mum."

I followed Sam's pointing finger and spotted Gabby's ragged fin with a hole in the middle as it sank below the water.

"And there's Bubble's daughter," continued Sam.

This time I saw a smooth shiny grey back arching and sinking in one graceful movement.

"What are they doing?" I asked Sam.

Sam looked up from his tape recorder and clicked the off button.

"It's hard to be sure," he replied. "But I reckon they've just met up and they're greeting one another."

I looked down into the water where the seagrass swayed and waved like undersea ribbons. The dolphins were stroking each other with their flippers. It certainly looked like a dolphin family get-together.

Then I saw Squeak. He was playing with Bubble, gliding over and under her as she swam around him. They were moving so fast I thought they'd get dizzy.

DIZZY DOLPHIN

Bubble's daughter is a beautiful young dolphin with a creamy belly and scarcely a scar, although she has got the same bent-over fin as her mum. Sam says she's about five years old.

I tugged Sam's arm.

"Sam," I pleaded. "I've got to swim with Bubble's daughter. Look, she's asking me to. Pleeeeese!"

It was true. Bubble's daughter was eyeing me with her mouth open. She was making a friendly clicking, buzzing sound.

Sam grinned, "I think she may be asking for a fish, but if you fancy a quick dip, go ahead."

One record-breaking quick-change act later I was splashing in the blue water.

The water glittered with light. Under the water, dim sunbeams shone on the white sand beneath my flippered feet.

All at once Squeak came charging up to play with me. Or at least I thought he was about to. But he zoomed past me, trailing bubbles. Behind me two more dolphins had appeared. I wasn't sure, but judging by Squeak's behaviour they must be his friend Nipper and Slap. All at once the baby dolphins were bumping and rolling belly up and leaping out of the water with excitement.

I laughed and swam towards Bubble's daughter. I wanted to get a picture of this pretty dolphin splashing in the warm blue water. And I did – in the end!

As I pointed my camera, the dolphin flipped out of the water, and sploshed back down. Then she flicked her tail up to dive. Her tail whacked a wave. SPLASH! It hit me in the face.

Splash, I thought. That just has to be your name!

SPLASH SPLASHING!

Splash spotted another dolphin swimming towards us. All at once she rushed off to tickle the newcomer with her flippers and roll around in an underwater somersault show.

It's wonderful how watching dolphins can help you figure out the links between them. The new dolphin was about the same size as Splash (and so probably the same age). I decided to take a closer look and swam slowly towards them. They were doing something with a piece of seagrass.

"That looks interesting," I said to myself. And so it proved...

Splash rose up with the seagrass wrapped over her flipper. She dived and, as she headed down, the seagrass fell off. But Splash caught the seaweed and passed it to her friend. Three times the dolphins took it in turns to dress up in the seagrass and pass it on.

SPLASH WITH SEAGRASS

"You've got to see this!" I called to Sam. "They're dressing up!"

"*What?*" called Sam. Stuck on the boat, he was missing the underwater show that was happening just a few metres from his nose.

I was just about to explain when I felt something nudge me from behind. Suddenly my legs were kicked up from under me by ... a dolphin diving between them!

Splash, gurgle, gurgle. My feet flew in the air and my head fell back. The snorkel dropped from my mouth and water went up my nose. I gasped and spluttered up to the surface with water spraying from my nostrils.

"Cheeky!" I called to the dolphin trickster. It was Splash's friend, and that's how she got her name!

I could have stayed in the water for ever, watching the dolphins rub and pet and play. I'd have happily turned into a dolphin myself if a fairy godmother had been handy with a wand and a spell. But Sam started looking at his watch and saying, "Come on, Daisy, we've got to make a move."

After I'd dried off I was still bubbling with the thrills and fun of the dolphins. But by the time we reached Monkey Mia I was ready for a shower, a snack and bed.

And I was still happy. I was so happy I felt like jumping for joy. "I wanna jump!" I sang. And then it struck me. But that's what dolphins do! Is my wish coming true? Am I really turning into a dolphin? I hope so!

## July 26

Today's dolphin adventure began this morning when the dolphins played their all-time favourite game…

All of a sudden there they were. Maybe they'd heard *Cindy*'s engine and come to us. This time they were swimming alongside the boat. I grabbed the side of the cabin and quickly edged along the ledge to *Cindy*'s front. From here, peering over the shiny metal rail, I got a grandstand view.

The dolphins were bow-riding. They were being pushed along by the water that was being pushed aside by our boat. Looking down into the rushing shining water, I saw Bubble, Squeak, Cheeky and Splash.

BOW-RIDING DOLPHINS

They were swimming at our speed and it felt like neither the boat nor the dolphins were moving. They could have been frozen in glass. The only things that proved otherwise were the bubbles bubbling from the dolphins' blowholes. All at once the dolphins came up to breathe. All together they phoofed a gasp of air … and all together they dived.

I noticed Squeak beat his tail extra quickly and edged into the lead in front of the boat. But Bubble rushed up and pushed him aside.

"You're a bit young for that kind of thing!" I imagined her snapping with a cross flick of her flippers.

"Daisy, can you hold the wheel?" called Sam from the cabin. "I want to take a look at this."

And that's why I missed the rest of the bow-riding. But what I had seen was magic!

Sam says dolphins bow-ride all the time, although I hadn't seen it before. No one knows why they hitch underwater rides (they also bow-ride beside whales, who get grumpy), but maybe being pulled along reminds dolphins of those happy days when they were babies and swam with their mums.

After a while Sam asked me to switch off *Cindy*'s engine and we drifted. We waited to see what the dolphins would do next. The dolphins stayed close to the boat. The youngsters played, and the older dolphins dozed happily in the warm bright sunshine. And so another incredible day passed...

## July 27

When we found the dolphins this morning I hoped we'd be in for another day of dozing and playing.

And that's just what happened, until the male dolphins showed up.

I saw them first, a line of three fins cutting through the water.

"Look, there's more!" I called to Sam, who had his eyes on our dolphins.

Sam swung his binoculars round and fiddled with the focus. "Yes, I see them," he said. "I think they're young males."

The males kept their distance, chasing and twisting and leaping in some private game. As we watched, two of our dolphins set off to join them.

"Cheeky and Splash," said Sam. "I thought as much!"

I had to ask Sam to talk me through which dolphins like to play together. I found out that Cheeky likes playing with the boys. And Splash tags along because she's Cheeky's best friend.

BUT BOYS ARE SO STUPID!

I'm calling the male dolphins Buzz, Rags and Smiler. They're one of the all-male groups Sam told me about. They're too young to mate, but in a few years' time they'll be chasing after females together.

Yes, being with dolphins is like watching a flippered soap opera … with fish thrown in!

## July 31

As ever, I'm a bit short of things to say about my dry-land days. The high point came this morning when the boy dolphins turned up to be fed. I got this picture...

BREAKFAST FOR BUZZ - AND SMILER AND RAGS!

Don't they look cheeky with their eager bright eyes and their greedy wide-open mouths? Typical boys!

## August 1

Today it all changed...

I felt that after last week's lovely dolphin days the dolphins had to be there for us. But they weren't. The glassy water stretched to the sky like a desert. We couldn't spot a single flipper.

*Where were the dolphins?*

We waited for two hours and suddenly I couldn't take it any more.

"Something's happened... Something's happened," I repeated and bit my lip. I knew Squeak was in danger. I could just *feel* it.

Sam's brow wrinkled as he gave me a puzzled look. "You can't be sure, Daisy. It's quite common for dolphins to move somewhere else. That's what dolphins do."

I nearly stamped my foot with rage. "Trust me, Sam," I hissed. My mind was rushing through all the terrible dangers that could hurt the dolphins. Sharks, poisonous fish, killer whales...

Somehow I talked Sam into looking for the dolphins. And just as the light was turning golden and the shadows were darkening on the red cliffs, I saw a dark shape lying on the sandy shore.

"DOLPHIN – OVER THERE!" I yelled.

I knew it was Bubble or Squeak. It had to be – I just *knew* it.

Sam steered the *Cindy* as close to the shore as he could. It was Bubble! I could see her bent-over fin with its circle of scratchy white scars. Further out I could make out a small fin circling in the calm water. It was Squeak.

Bubble wasn't moving. She was clearly in desperate trouble. *Was she even alive?*

"She's stranded," said Sam.

I'd already guessed what had happened. Dolphins are designed to swim in water. But on land they're helpless.

## DAISY'S DOLPHIN NOTES
### STRANDED DOLPHINS

1. A dolphin can get stuck on dry land for lots of reasons...

• They are chasing a fish onto a beach and go too far.

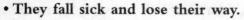

• They get caught on a beach as the tide goes out.

• They fall sick and lose their way.

2. Getting stranded can land a dolphin in terrible danger.

• Unable to escape, the dolphin can be attacked by other animals.

• Their skin quickly dries out and the dolphin can suffer painful sunburn.

• Dolphin bodies are suited to the cool sea –

a layer of fat called "blubber" under their skin keeps them warm. But they can't stay cool in air. On a hot day, a dolphin will soon die from the heat.

I leapt into the shallow water and splashed over to Bubble. She was still breathing. I could hear each wheezy breath from her blowhole. Her sad dull eyes widened as she saw me.

I bent over her, talking breathlessly. "You're all right," I said. "We're here. I want to help you."

Gently, I touched Bubble's side. Her skin felt hot and dry and I could feel her heart beating. It was racing.

And then Sam arrived. He was carrying a bundle. It was the grubby tarpaulin cover that he throws over *Cindy*'s deck in wet weather. Quickly he bent over and dumped the sheet in the sea. Next he pulled off his shirt and soaked it too. Sam splashed over to Bubble and held the shirt over her. Water dripped and splashed down the dolphin's sides.

Bubble opened her mouth weakly and smacked her tail softly on the sand. She was panting like a hot, sick dog. Sam crouched beside her. He was staring into Bubble's mouth.

"There are no ulcers or sores," he said. "That's a good sign. And she doesn't look sick. Take off your watch and ring. We'll try to get Bubble into the water. You can't have anything on your hands that could cut her flesh."

"Hear that?" I whispered to Bubble. "We're going to help you."

I slipped the watch off my wrist and put it together with my ring in the pocket of my shorts.

The mother dolphin feebly flapped her tail.

"Keep clear of her tail and teeth," warned Sam. "She could still hurt you."

I stood back as Sam gently dripped some more water over Bubble's body all the way up from her tired tail to her suffering snout.

"Take over, Daisy," said Sam. "I'm going to get the tarpaulin. Don't drop anything in her blowhole. Water in her breathing tubes could drown her even on dry land."

Fearfully I took Sam's heavy wet shirt and began to drip water on Bubble's sides. The clear drops ran down her hot grey body. Sam dragged the heavy tarpaulin up the beach and spread it beside the stranded dolphin.

"If we can get her onto the sheet, we might be able to drag her into the water. But it's going to be hard – she's very heavy."

"We've got to try!" I said. "We've got to!"

Then I bent low over Bubble and talked quietly to her.

"You've got to help us," I told Bubble.

I gently touched the dolphin's side and she twitched suddenly. Her tail swung and she slipped sideways in the sand. She was half on the sheet already!

"Do it again," urged Sam.

"Come on, Bubble!" I said.

In the distance I could hear Squeak whistling furiously. He sounds scared, I thought. Maybe he's calling her. I touched Bubble again, and once more she jerked. This time her whole body slid onto the sheet!

"Well done, Bubble!" I gasped with delight.

"Quick, grab the tarpaulin!" ordered Sam.

I hooked my fingers through the metal ring in the side of the wet sheet.

"Ready?" asked Sam. "OK, and HEAVE … HEAVE!"

The tarpaulin shifted a little. Bubble screeched with alarm and her whole body jerked as she began to move.

"It's OK," I soothed. "We're going to get you back in the water."

"HEAVE!" called Sam again.

And I heaved with all my might. I heaved with all the strength in my big shoulders. I heaved until my knuckles turned white and my shoulders shook.

Slowly, heavily the tarpaulin shifted with Bubble aboard. First her tail dipped into the salty water. A moment later a little wave licked along her side.

Her tail jerked and slapped.

Now it was in the water the tarpaulin dragged less.

"HEAVE!" shouted Sam again.

Once more I pulled for Bubble and Squeak. The water lapped around Bubble's back, her flippers splashed.

"We've got to turn her around," said Sam. "She's facing the wrong way. Pull her round this way. Come on, HEAVE!"

But Bubble could hear Squeak's cries for help and they guided her. Her body wriggled from side to side, her flippers beat the water as she slowly turned.

As Sam and I tugged the tarpaulin around with one last heave, the mother dolphin pulled herself forward into deeper water. At last Bubble was swimming!

There were tears in my eyes as I watched Squeak rush up to his mum and nuzzle her. He was screeching with excitement, until his lungs were fit to burst.

"We've done it!" I cried, blinking back tears of joy.

"Yes," gasped Sam. "She's swimming, at least."

He wiped the sweat off his brow. He really cares about dolphins, I thought. And he's quite a hero!

WHAT A HERO!

"She will be OK, won't she?" I asked anxiously.

Sam watched the mother and baby dolphin swim away into the bright blue bay.

"I *hope* so," he said tiredly. "But we don't know how long Bubble's been lying there. If she's got bad sunburn then she could be too ill to hunt. And that means Squeak will die. We may have got here too late..."

# DANCING WITH DOLPHINS

## *August 2*

I sat on the jetty waiting for Sam. It promised to be a lovely day of blue skies and gentle seas, but the thoughts boiling and bubbling away in my brain were far from lovely. Was Bubble OK? Was Squeak safe?

I stared grimly at the blue sky. As I looked away, a pelican flapped lazily across the bay. I could see its feathered shape reflecting in the still water.

Just then a dolphin threw itself into the air. It shone like a shiny metal toy in the morning sun, then it dived into the water and ripples spread out in all directions. Was it Bubble?

Frantically I rummaged in my bag for my binoculars. I tore off the lens caps and put the binoculars to my eyes. Where was the dolphin now?

Surely it would leap again?! It did. But not where I'd expected to see it.

I heard the distant splash and turned just in time to see the dolphin's tail disappear into the water. Just then another smaller dolphin leapt from the water just behind the first one. Was it a baby? I let out a gasp of excitement. Could it have been Squeak?

I just wasn't sure.

My arms felt heavy from holding the binoculars but I didn't dare stop looking. I was still gripping the binoculars when Sam arrived.

We looked all day but saw no trace of Bubble and Squeak. We spent much of the time chatting and sometimes daydreaming as the water lapped against *Cindy*'s sides and the sun made dazzle patterns on the sea. The day was as warm as it had promised to be. But I couldn't enjoy it until I was sure Bubble and Squeak were OK. And that's why I wrote these gloomy notes...

## DAISY'S DOLPHIN NOTES
### DAMAGE TO DOLPHINS

1. Dolphin skin breaks easily. But because dolphins live in water their wounds can't dry into dry crusty scabs like human wounds.

2. Some of the dolphin's flesh dies and hardens to keep germs out – but this

**protection doesn't always work. Germs can make a dolphin sick.**

**3. Dolphins can fall sick if they get too many parasites. These are creatures such as wriggling worms that live in a dolphin's guts.**

**4. All in all, it's tough being a dolphin and it's no wonder that many of them live less than 25 years in the wild.**

And then, just as we turned to head home, Sam spotted two dark specks in the distance. They were cutting v-shaped ripples in the still water. Was it? Could it be? IT WAS! Bubble and Squeak were back!

"THEY'RE SAFE!" I yelled and gave Sam a great big hug.

"Hmm, they look well enough," said Sam, rubbing his beard, "but I think Bubble's got a touch of sunburn."

There on Bubble's back was an ugly white splotch where the skin had peeled.

"Oooh that looks painful!" I cried.

Dolphins are so strong and so alive, it's shocking to think how easily they can get injured.

BUBBLE'S SUNBURN

## *August 3*

If I was a dolphin and I'd been stranded and sunburned, I'd be resting. Come to think of it, I'd have swum to the nearest vet for emergency treatment and a gallon of suntan lotion!

But not Bubble! When we found her this morning she was leaping and splashing and playing with Squeak and Splash. Only the sore white patch was there to remind us of her near-fatal accident.

Suddenly Splash made the biggest leap I'd ever seen. She seemed to float in the empty air, arching her sleek and shiny grey body. It was so incredible that I shouted to Sam in the cabin.

"Come and see this!"

Sam looked up from his map as Splash hit the water and a wave broke against the cabin window. The rest of the wave splashed over me.

"WOW!" I gasped. I wiped the water from my eyes and dripping hair. Wow indeed! And that was just the start. As I sat in the hot sun with my legs dangling over the front of the boat, Splash put on an incredible free show.

Once more she shot into the blue sky and this time she twisted and flipped, head over tail, hitting the bay in a wet white explosion of noise and spray and water. Nothing on Earth. I repeat *nothing* can prepare you for it. You've just got to see it! And if you're thinking, oh there goes Daisy getting carried away again, just look at these pictures!

SPLASH THE SUPERSTAR!

Have you ever seen anything so exciting?

And that got me thinking. Why do dolphins put so much effort into leaping around? Why do they bother? I knew I couldn't rest until I'd found out the answer. So I've been looking through my dolphin books...

# DAISY'S DOLPHIN NOTES
## SWIMMING AND LEAPING

1. A dolphin can swim at 5 km per hour with a top speed of about 35 km per hour. This may sound slow, but it's hard to swim fast because the water slows you down. Even so,

a dolphin's usual swimming speed is as fast as a human Olympic champion. And the dolphin does it *without even trying.*

2. Unlike fish, who swim by beating their tails from side to side, dolphins move their tails up and down.

3. A dolphin's streamlined shape allows it to slip through water. Its smooth skin is always rubbing off, making it hard for shellfish such as barnacles to steal a free ride.

SO LONG!

4. Dolphins often leap to go faster since it's less effort to fly through the air than to swim through the water.

5. Leaping is also a way for a dolphin to have fun and show off to its dolphin friends.

As we sail back to Monkey Mia, Sam and I often chat about the day. We like to chew over the things we've seen and laugh at the dolphins' tricks. But not today. For once even a champion chatterbox like me was quiet. All I could think of was Splash and her gob-smacking, gravity-defying, lovely leaping.

## *August 8*

The dolphins were further out today, playing in the deeper water. Sam said we were in a deep channel in Shark Bay's maze of seagrass banks and sandy shallows.

Watching the dolphins dive and rise up in the clear shining water was too much for me. I wanted to be in there too – and I soon was!

At first, as my head bobbed above the surface, all I could see was the dark blue sea. In this deep, cooler water, the waves rose and fell like liquid hills and valleys.

I dropped my head under the surface and saw sunbeams like shafts of sunshine in a dusty room. Dark dots whooshed through the water. I could hear clicks and whistles and in seconds the dolphins were around me, gliding and rushing and trailing bubbles.

I spun round. I felt like an underwater dancer – but I probably looked like an underwater frog. Then I turned again and again. As I watched, the dolphins dived into the shadowy deep. I waited and waited for them to reappear under the water until my breathless body was shouting and gulping for air.

"LET ME BREATHE! LET ME BREATHE!" shouted my lungs.

"Yes, breathe, Daisy. You can't hold your breath as long as a dolphin!" I reminded myself.

Afterwards I found out how dolphins can hold their breath for so much longer than me…

## DAISY'S DOLPHIN NOTES
### DIVING DOLPHINS

1. A dolphin's life is made up of breathing and diving so it's not too surprising that they're good at holding their breath and diving. In fact they're very, very, VERY good!

2. Take a deep breath. Keep breathing in until you can't fit another puff of air into your lungs – now let it out. That might have felt like a lot of air, but it was probably only one-tenth of the air your lungs can hold. A baby dolphin can breathe EIGHT TIMES more air with a single breath! And, what's more, each breathtaking breath takes just a split second!

**3. Can you imagine breathing through a hole in the top of your head like a dolphin?** Just before the dolphin reaches the air, it snorts out a snotty watery spray from the dip its blowhole sits in. The spray flies out faster than you can sneeze.

SQUIRT SPLASH

**4. Incredibly, unlike your breathing, which carries on when you're not thinking about it – a dolphin has to remember to breathe!** If a dolphin gets knocked out, it stops breathing … and dies.

I showed Sam my notes.

"Yeah sure, that's all true," he said, speaking loudly above the throbbing engine. "But there's more. Imagine being in the water. You know how it presses all around you?"

I nodded.

Sam carefully polished his glasses. "Well, the deeper you go the harder the water squeezes. Humans need special equipment to dive below 50 metres. And dolphins mostly don't go as deep. But they can dive seven times deeper – nearly one kilometre there and back on just one breath of air!"

"That's impossible!" I gasped. I imagined Squeak beating his little tail as he swam down, down, down into the dark empty depths of the ocean.

OH-ER!

"Not for a dolphin," smiled Sam. "Their bodies are designed for pressure. Their lungs squash flat and they store the oxygen they need to stay alive in their blood and muscles. Mind you, coming up from that depth is the same as if you were to run up all 1,576 stairs to the top of the Empire State Building … while holding your breath!"

I laughed. Now that's a fact I didn't know!

## *August 9*

Today, when we set off from the jetty in the dawn mist, I had high hopes of another day of diving with dolphins.

But I was disappointed.

First the mist was slow to lift and we had trouble finding the dolphins. Then, when at last we spotted them, they were all floating gently in the water. I could see Bubble, Squeak, Gabby and Splash, and all of them were bobbing lazily, heads up and tails down, in the long gentle ripples.

"Looks like they're snagging," said Sam. "We've seen it before with the adults."

*Snacking?* I thought. I pictured Bubble helping herself from a big bag of fish-flavoured crisps. But the dolphins weren't eating!

Sam saw my puzzled frown and came to my rescue.

"It's kind of like sleeping except the dolphins are always half-awake."

"Half-awake?"

"Yeah, dolphins need to be awake to breathe. And anyway, it's not a good idea to go to sleep when there's hungry sharks and orcas about. So the dolphins don't sleep. They just shut down half their brain at a time." Every day I find out something new about dolphins. Something weird. Something wonderful.

"So dolphins never, ever sleep?" I asked.

"Not properly," said Sam. "Just look at their eyes."

By now the boat was drifting on the tide like the dolphins. I leant over the rail along *Cindy*'s front and took a close look at Bubble, the nearest dolphin. One of her eyes was lazily half-open and the other was closed.

BUBBLE SNAGGING

"You'd best not swim today," said Sam. "The dolphins need their rest and they won't want to be disturbed."

I nodded. I did want to swim with the dolphins, I really did. But I cared for them enough not to put my wishes in front of their need for sleep. It's only fair – no one likes to be bothered when they're resting. Even if they're only half-asleep!

## August 10

The storm came in the night as unexpectedly as a burglar. The first thing I knew about it was the noise. I was having a dream about a dolphin orchestra. Bubble and Squeak and their friends were all part of it. Bubble was playing a metal plate rack, Splash was playing a violin with a car aerial and Squeak was banging a drainpipe with a teaspoon.

Then I woke up. But Squeak was still playing! Oh no he wasn't! It was the wire ropes on a nearby boat banging together in the wind.

Yes, it really was windy. I could hear the THWACK, THWACK! of tent flaps whacking open and shut and the roar and hiss of big waves hitting the beach.

Outside some people were shouting. Something about the boats... The boat! Sam's sleeping on the boat tonight! Was he all right?

Shivering, I scrambled into my clothes and stumbled outside into the gale. My hair blew into my eyes and the stinging sand blew against my legs. Then I heard a horrible RASPING RIPPING TEARING sound as a tent crashed down.

Screwing up my eyes against the wind, I saw boats diving and dipping and rocking and heaving in the crazy bay. One boat was actually upside-down! Only its cable stopped the waves from sweeping it away.

A dripping figure rushed up to me. It was Sam!

"Are you all right?" I cried. "Where's the boat?"

"Tied-up and anchored!" shouted Sam. "Are you OK?"

I nodded, shivering.

ARE YOU OK?

"Right," he yelled. "We'd better get your stuff out of the caravan. This could be a cyclone!"

A cyclone! I thought desperately. A tropical storm that smashes caravans, wrecks towns and kills people.

Sam helped me to stuff a few things into my rucksack – binoculars, diary, clothes, books, food, water. If the storm smashed the caravan, my belongings could be blown into the bay and I wanted to hang on to a few vital bits. Already the caravan was rocking and shaking in the wind.

As we threw open the caravan door the cold rain hit us, stinging our faces, soaking us through and through.

"In here!" shouted Sam with rain streaming off his glasses. He half-pushed and half-dragged me into the toilets. "They're solidly built. They shouldn't blow down," he gasped.

Leaning tiredly against the washbasins was a family of visitors.

"What a holiday!" moaned the mum.

"We'll be all right, won't we?" asked the little girl, and her little brother began to cry in sympathy.

"Course we'll be fine!" said the mum crouching down and putting her arms around the children.

"I'm off to see if anyone needs help," said Sam.

"Want any help, mate?" asked the dad.

"Sure," said Sam.

...e two men walked out into the howling
...e again, Sam was the hero of the hour!

...oved to be a long, dark, chilly, noisy, scary
night. Have you ever slept in a toilet? Take it from me
– it's smelly, it's uncomfortable and it's grim. When
Sam came back I was doubled up on the concrete
floor. My tired head was on my knees and my aching
arms were wrapped around my stiff legs.

"It's over!" said Sam, gently touching my shoulder.

We staggered outside like a pair of beaten-up
boxers. I rubbed my eyes in the dim morning light.
The wind had stopped and Sam and I headed down
to the beach.

But what beach? During the night a nasty
magician had turned the beach into a big heap of
seagrass and smashed-up wood and tangled rope.

DISASTER!

And further out, beside the muddy seagrass banks laid bare by the tide, were the boats. Some were floating upside-down, others had sunk. One boat looked like a giant had taken a bite from its cabin.

But where was *Cindy*?

"There she is!" I cried. "Thank goodness she's still floating!"

Sam dashed into the water. *Cindy* was floating sure enough, but she was rolling too. She must have taken in a lot of water.

I glanced at the end of the beach. Everything in the bay seemed to have been washed up by the waves and smashed on the shore. And then a horrible, horrible thought rushed through my brain.

"Oh no!" I cried desperately. "What about the dolphins?"

# STRANGE SOUNDS

## *August 12*

The storm has changed everything. The laid-back holiday village of Monkey Mia is now a laid-low village of battered caravans and broken boats. Some tents have been blown away and their contents scattered to the winds. Luckily, my caravan is still standing.

But right in the middle of this miserable muddle Superman and Superwoman have come to our rescue. Yes, Clyde and Cheryl have been brilliant –

LOOKS LIKE THESE FOLKS NEED US!

leading the hunt for lost belongings, nailing down torn-up roofs and handing out mugs of tea, coffee and hot chocolate.

I've been helping too.

"We don't get too many cyclones," said Cheryl cheerfully. "This one was just a flick of a cat's paw. I heard there was one back in 1979 that lifted a fishing boat into the caravan site. Now that *was* a storm!"

But when will I see Bubble and Squeak again? I don't know. The water damaged *Cindy*'s engine and Sam had her towed back to Denham for repairs.

I'm really gutted. I feel like grinding my teeth because I'm stuck on the shore instead of diving with dolphins. Oh well, at least I've got plenty here to keep me busy.

## *August 15*

With the boat needing (what else?) spare parts from Perth, I'm left high and dry. But while I'm waiting for *Cindy* to be fixed, I've got myself a job. Cheryl wants me to do a talk at the dolphin information centre. The only problem is the subject she's asked me to speak on.

"I don't know anything about dolphin senses," I protested.

Cheryl shrugged. "I don't suppose the visitors know much either. But it's a fascinating topic. I'd love to do it if I had the time. I'm *sure* you'll come up with something good, Daisy."

And maybe I could, I thought. When I set my mind to something I'm a determined lady! I've got my dolphin books. They sit on the shelf in my caravan neatly arranged in order of author's name (well, I am a librarian…). And if I get stuck, Sam's just a phone call away.

So that's what I've been doing – diving into the strange world of dolphin senses. And here's what I've found out…

## DAISY'S DOLPHIN NOTES
### DOLPHIN SENSES

1. Dolphin eyes see well in air and water. Special tears protect the eyes from the salty water.

2. Dolphin ears are tiny holes. They may hear some sounds but a dolphin hears best underwater through its lower jaw! The jaw feels shockwaves made by underwater sounds.

3. Dolphins make clicks in the breathing passages in their heads. The sounds bounce off objects and the echoes come back to the dolphin. The echoes tell a dolphin the size and distance of the object. This is known as echolocation.

SMALL LUNCH AT 2 METRES

HA HA HA HA

4. Dolphin skin is sensitive to touch and temperature.

5. Dolphins can taste their fishy food but they like different tastes to us.

For some reason dolphins quite like the sour taste of lemon juice.

6. Dolphins have no sense of smell.

The most amazing thing of all is the way dolphins use echoes to "see" with sound. Imagine Bubble tracking a fish. Somehow, and scientists aren't sure how, she makes clicks in her breathing passages. Inside her head are strange structures called the "melon" and "monkey lips" that turn the sound into a narrow beam like a torch light.

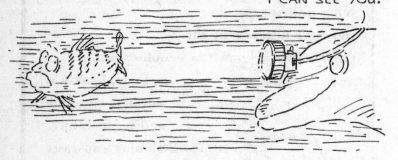

CLICK! The sound hits a fish and bounces back as an echo. It's like shouting into an echoey tunnel and hearing your own voice. *Click!* Bubble hears the echo rushing through her jaw. Hungrily, Bubble tracks the echo. As Bubble closes on the fish she clicks higher and faster, hundreds of times a second. She clicks so fast and so high that we can't hear her. She turns her head to measure how the fish is moving. Now she's like a whizzing guided missile, locked onto its target. And CRUNCH, SLAPPITY-GULP! – she's caught a tasty fish supper!

That's amazing enough. But what really sends shivers down my spine is what Bubble "sees" with her echolocation. You see, sound doesn't just bounce off a fish, it bounces off its insides too. And it doesn't just work with fish – it works with people! Every time I've dived with dolphins I've felt a funny feeling like a tingle running through my body. And now I'm sure it's Bubble and Squeak eyeing up my wobbly insides!

### *August 18*

All the time I've been helping repair storm damage and reading about dolphin senses, I've been wondering whether Bubble and Squeak made it through the storm. Of course, I haven't been able to go and look for them with Sam. But whenever I've had a chance I've been down on the jetty talking to boat owners and fishermen.

"Have you seen a mother and baby dolphin?" I ask as I show them my photo of Bubble and Squeak. But they only shake their heads dumbly.

"Take another look," I urge them. But so far no one's seen anything.

Until this morning…

I was sitting on the end of the jetty with my legs dangling into space. For the umpteenth time I was wondering what had become of the dolphins. And at that very moment a shiny grey shape whizzed through the water, followed quickly by two more. I was too far away to get a good view but from what I could see of their dorsal fins, I guessed they must be Splash, Gabby and Bubble.

The girls were back in town!

A moment later I spotted a small shape trailing in the water close to the last dolphin. It had to be Squeak – he was alive!

WAIT FOR ME!

I brushed the hair out of my eyes and let out a scream of delight. I was so happy I raced back along the jetty and leapt onto the beach. I ran wildly with the sand jumping about my legs and my arms spread wide like a jumbo jet.

"It's good to be alive!" I sang. And then I noticed a small group of tourists watching me with interest.

"Just being happy!" I called to them. And what's wrong with that? I thought.

## *August 20*

Well, I've done my dolphin talk and I tell you it's the bravest thing I've ever done. Yes, I know I'll try anything, but doing talks really isn't my thing!

"You'll be fine!" Clyde reassured me.

I peeped through the door at the audience. The room was packed. My heart started to thump.

"Control yourself, Daisy," I gulped. "They're only people, and you like chatting with people."

I gripped my pile of papers in my sweaty hands. I had written out the whole talk. I only had to read it word for word.

Clyde held the door open. Everyone turned to look at me. I felt their eyes watching me as I followed him to the front of the crowd. My heart was leaping like a kangaroo. I hardly heard Clyde introduce me.

"Ladies and gentleman," I began in a squeaky voice, "dolphins make the strangest sounds…"

A very little boy in the front row was watching me with interest. Suddenly he stuck up his hand. I felt like I was back in school.

"Yes?" I asked the boy.

"What sort of sounds?" said the boy.

"Well," I said, "there's one that sounds like Buzzzzzzzzzzzzzzzzzz!"

A few people laughed.

"And there's one that sounds like clicking," I said, feeling encouraged. And I began to click my tongue, *click, click, click...*

BUZZZ...
CLICK!

By now most of the audience was chuckling and a few of the children were trying to make the sounds themselves.

"Of course," I said, "some of the most complex sounds dolphins make are whistles. I'm not sure if I can do them..."

"Oh, go on – try!" urged the boy's mum.

"OK, here goes," I said, beginning to relax...

The hour passed very speedily as I went through all the different sounds I'd heard dolphins make. Sometimes I asked children from the audience to make the sounds. There was no shortage of willing volunteers! But although I found time for a few words on dolphin senses and echolocation, I didn't look at my notes once.

At the end the audience clapped loudly and one or two people even cheered!

"Can't you make some more sounds?" asked the little boy.

## *August 21*

I'm getting used to grinning people coming up to me and saying "Great talk, Daisy! I loved the sound effects!" But now I've got something new to think about. At last *Cindy* is ready! And this time it's going to be different.

"We're not going at dawn," said Sam on the phone last night. "I'm writing an article about how dolphins keep in touch at night. How do you feel about a night cruise?"

It sounded exciting. "When do we go?" I asked.

## *August 23*

I've spent much of today sleeping, but I'm not going to eat until I've told you about last night.

Yesterday evening the bay was still and the boats sat quietly in the water. You wouldn't think that two weeks ago it had been so staggeringly stormy.

As we set off, the sun set behind the cliffs and everything — clouds, sea and even the sides of our boat – turned a soft golden colour. At first there was no sign of any dolphins. On and on we tracked, further out into the darkening bay. Then, when it was completely dark, Sam switched off the engine and threw the anchor overboard with a dull, heavy splash.

"Let's see what we can hear," he said.

He dropped an underwater microphone into the water. Carefully, he put on a pair of earphones and then picked up his tape recorder and switched it on.

"Ah yes," he said into the tape recorder. "There they are! Bubble's nearby, I can hear her."

"You can hear Bubble?" I cried. "How do you know it's her?"

Sam couldn't hear me, but I guessed that he knows the dolphins well enough to recognize their calls. Every dolphin has a special whistle that it learns from its mum. The whistle means something like "Hi, it's me, Bubble!" And once you know it, you can tell the dolphin is nearby.

As Sam listened to the dolphins, I gazed over the boat's side. The bay was completely dark and the water and sky were as black as a deep, dark well.

It was so dark that you couldn't see where water ended and sky began. All I could see were the glittering stars reflecting on the water like tiny pearls. Above us was the ghostly glow of the Milky Way with its billions of faint faraway stars. I felt as if we were floating on an ocean of stars.

"Hey, Daisy," whispered Sam, "have a listen…"

Slowly I put on the earphones and closed my eyes. For a second I felt as if I was underwater. I could hear the soft sounds of grains of sand rubbing and small stones clicking and fish grunting. And there was the distant sigh of waves on a faraway beach. This was the dolphin's world and this is what they heard too.

Then I heard clicks and splashes. Sure enough there were dolphins out there. I could hear their yelps and pops and squeals. Some sounds reminded me of musical instruments – well, sort of. I imagined a vicious violin torturing a cowardly cello. Or a scary saxophone picking on a frightened flute. I'd heard underwater dolphin sounds before, but never this clearly.

"Wow!" I said to Sam as I handed him the earphones. "It's like nothing on Earth!"

Sam nodded.

"Yeah," he agreed. "If only we understood what it all means. At present we've only got a basic idea."

Basic idea or not, I just have to tell you what's known about dolphin language...

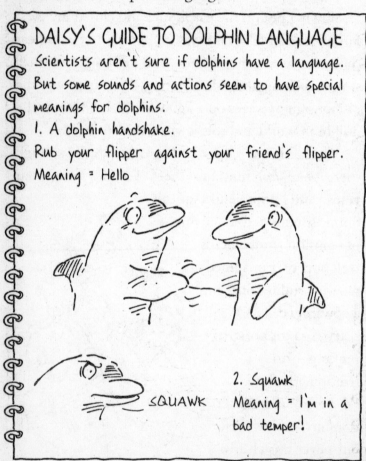

DAISY'S GUIDE TO DOLPHIN LANGUAGE

Scientists aren't sure if dolphins have a language. But some sounds and actions seem to have special meanings for dolphins.

1. A dolphin handshake.
Rub your flipper against your friend's flipper.
Meaning = Hello

SQUAWK

2. Squawk
Meaning = I'm in a bad temper!

3. Blowing bubbles from your blowhole
Little bubbles = I'm playing

Lots of big bubbles = I'M CROSS!

4. Chirp
Meaning = Hi, buddy!

5. Scream
Meaning = I'm excited!

After a while Sam said that the dolphins had moved away and it was time to head home. I wasn't too sorry. The chilly night air made me shiver and I began to think longingly of my warm cosy sleeping bag. Of course, it was back in the caravan.

## *August 25*

Listening to dolphins has left me wondering how clever they are. We talked about it today. And we've had plenty of time for talking. The dolphins didn't show up today or yesterday.

"Are dolphins really as smart – or even smarter than humans?" I asked Sam.

Sam didn't think so. "Hmm, tests show they're about as smart as apes," he said.

I wasn't so sure. "But dolphins have such big brains," I protested. "Don't they understand what we are saying?"

"I'm not sure if they understand actual words," said Sam. "Dolphins can learn a sort of sign language from their trainer. They can even make sense of a command like "take ball to hoop" – and know that it's different to "take hoop to ball…""

"So they *are* clever!" I said.

Sam scratched his beard thoughtfully.

"We just don't know enough about how their brains work to say how clever they are. But they're smart enough to use tools. Round here they use sponges – the sea animals that get made into bath sponges – to 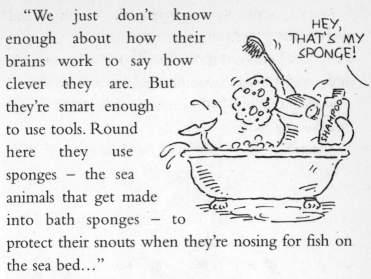 protect their snouts when they're nosing for fish on the sea bed…"

Sam stopped to polish his glasses.

"Maybe we're not clever enough to know how clever they are!" I said firmly. That's me, determined Daisy, always wanting the last word!

## August 26

WOW – what an honour – I just feel so good today! And the reason for this celebration? I've finally been allowed to feed the dolphins!

Cheryl asked me this morning. "It's a special thank you," she said, "for helping after the storm. And of course, for cheering us up with your dolphin talk!"

So there I was, complete with little-boy helper, feeding the dolphins.

Gabby, Splash and Cheeky lay in the sunny, shallow water with open mouths.

I picked a fish from the boy's bucket. It felt warm and slimy and heavy. As I crouched beside Gabby, the ripe fishy smell drifted up my nostrils and made me wrinkle my nose.

"Here's a fish," I told her. "Are you hungry?"

MY MOMENT OF GLORY!

It may have been my imagination but I was sure Gabby nodded. A moment later the dolphin grabbed the fish in its jaws and gulped it down. That's how dolphins eat. Their teeth can't chew – they're only used for grabbing fish.

Feeding the dolphins was the most exciting moment yet. I felt I was giving them something – the fish. And the dolphins were giving me something back – their trust.

# DAISY'S DOLPHIN NOTES
## DOLPHIN DINNERS

1. Dolphins are part of a big network of animals that live in Shark Bay and depend on each other for food. Scientists call this a "food web". It works something like this. The arrows show who eats who.

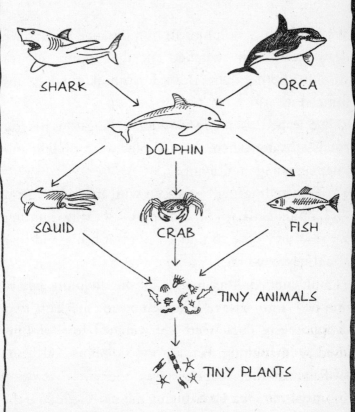

SHARK

ORCA

DOLPHIN

SQUID

CRAB

FISH

TINY ANIMALS

TINY PLANTS

2. Dolphins need to eat lots of fish. An adult dolphin will eat up to 90 small fish a day.

**3. Dolphins get most of the water they need from fish, but their skin also lets water soak into their body. The skin keeps out harmful salt that would make them ill if they had too much.**

## *August 30*

We spotted the dolphins from a distance and, as we drew near, Sam switched off the engine so we wouldn't bother them. But I don't think the dolphins noticed us.

We leaned over *Cindy's* side, looking towards the patch of water where the dolphins were circling and turning, rising and diving.

"They're hunting!" said Sam with an excited grin. "It's quite hard to find dolphins actually hunting because they have to find a school of fish – and that could be anywhere."

Suddenly another piece of the dolphin jigsaw dropped into place. I remembered the last two disappointing days when we searched for dolphins and found nothing. Perhaps the dolphins had been away hunting?

I tried the idea on Sam.

"Maybe," he said. "Maybe not. With dolphins you can never be sure."

Just then two of the dolphins leapt from the water. I saw the splashes catching the sunlight and shimmering into tiny rainbows.

"They're signalling," said Sam. "The splashes are telling every dolphin within ear-shot that there are fish to be caught."

It certainly worked! More dolphins began to appear, swimming fast and hungrily with scarcely a splash.

Suddenly I saw the fish leaping from the water, darting and flickering over the waves. Above us, the gulls screeched and soared, eager to grab their share. Underwater, I knew the dolphins were circling the fish, forcing them into an ever-tighter ball.

FEEDING TIME!

The dolphins were politely taking it in turns to dive amongst the fish and grab a few with a single bite. Part of me longed to dive with the dolphins and get a better view. But I knew I mustn't risk putting the dolphins off. They needed to feed in order to stay alive, and a nosy human was sure to get in their way.

As I watched, I spotted one dorsal fin rising in the bright water. A bent-over fin with a circle of scars and a white patch on the dolphin's back.

"Look, there's Bubble!" I shouted.

When Bubble came up again she had a floppy flapping fish in her mouth. And if she was getting her breakfast, I was sure that Squeak would be fed too.

"It's a yellow-tail," said Sam. "They're really bony fish – but dolphins love them!"

With that, Sam clambered along the edge of the boat. Leaning over the front rail, he gave me a running commentary…

"Look over there, Daisy!" It looks like the dolphins have trapped some of the fish just under the surface. That's a classic dolphin trick. And can you see that dolphin swimming on his back? He's actually chasing a yellowtail. On his back, the dolphin can get a better view of what's going on in front of his nose."

DOLPHIN BACKSTROKE

Sam was interrupted by an especially loud splash from the other side of the boat. Quickly Sam scrambled over to see what was happening.

"Ah, as I thought," he called. "One of the dolphins has just whacked a fish over the head with its tail to stun it. I reckon the stunned fish has already been eaten!"

For us, and the dolphins, it was a great day. But at last the fish escaped and the full-of-fish dolphins went their separate ways. Feeling tired, and a little sunburned, we decided to head home.

But then, out of a clear blue sea, disaster struck.

"Look!" I shouted to Sam. "There's something wrong with Squeak!"

I had spotted Squeak swimming nearby and there was something trailing behind him.

Now I could see it clearly in the water. It looked like a fishing line. A fishing line wrapped around Squeak's dorsal fin.

"OH!" I let out a little sob of dismay.

Where there was a fishing line there was almost certainly a fishing hook. There could be a sharp pointed hook stuck in Squeak's belly.

Squeak came up and squealed in pain. Bubble was circling anxiously and must have called to him because a second later the two dolphins rushed off at top speed.

"We've got to go after them!" I cried. "Squeak needs help!"

Sam looked at me and shook his head. His expression was grim. "We can't!" he said. "It's too late!"

Sam was right. Already the dolphins had left us far behind, dodging wildly from side to side, blindly rushing away in their panic.

What would happen to them? I wondered. Would the dolphins swim and swim until they were too weak and hungry to swim any more? And when the dolphins were tired out would the tiger sharks come for them? Would Squeak die because some stupid fisherman was too lazy to reel in a tangled fishing line?

# DOLPHINS IN DANGER

## *August 31*

Last night things got even worse...

I was steering the boat back to Monkey Mia when Sam gave me a sheepish look and said, "I know this isn't a good time – but I've got something to tell you."

I turned to look at him.

"I've got a big article to write," he continued. "It's a bit of a rush job. Well, it wasn't meant to be, but my computer has been a bit poorly – I think a cockroach got inside it. Anyway, it's fixed now, but there's only a couple of days left for the article."

My heart sank faster than a diving dolphin. "So you want to head *home*?" I asked fiercely. "After all this? But what about Squeak?" I gripped the polished wooden wheel until my knuckles gleamed.

Sam looked at the floor and nodded unhappily. "Look," he said. "I don't want to. Maybe I could stay an extra night on the boat and head home tomorrow. If you come with me, we could search for Squeak on the way."

"OK," I sighed. Anything was better than being stuck helpless on the shore.

This morning I looked at myself in the mirror. I've changed a lot in the last few months. My skin is tanned and freckled and I feel fit and strong from all my diving with dolphins. My hair is long and wild and lighter from the sunshine. And inside I've changed too. I'm happier and stronger. I wanted to be strong enough to believe that Squeak was OK.

"He'll be all right," I told my reflection. "Maybe he wasn't hurt too badly."

Dolphins with hooks stuck in them sometimes come to humans for help. Perhaps they can sense that we want to help them. Would Bubble and Squeak come back to us?

"We've got to find him today!" I told my frowning reflection. "We've just got to!"

Down at the jetty the wind was picking up. The whole bay was full of splashes and swirling, slurping waves. But the sky was clear and empty except for the faint shimmering white trail of a faraway jet. The boats danced on the water to the music of the wind twanging their wire ropes. With all these waves it would be hard to spot a dolphin's fin.

It was a tense morning, and in the end we didn't find the dolphins – they found us! Just like magic, suddenly there they were, riding our bow wave.

"THEY'RE HERE! THEY'RE HERE!" I yelled in excitement. And for one happy moment Squeak whooshed belly up in the shiny water. I saw that the hook had fallen out. He was safe! And to celebrate I sang "Baby's coming back!" to him.

LOOK, NO HOOK!

## September 1

Last night I travelled back to Monkey Mia by taxi, leaving Sam tapping away at his computer. After my day on the boat I wanted an early night, but my bed-time reading proved far from relaxing. The fishing-hook business had left me wondering about the dangers that dolphins face from humans. Sam leant me a book on the subject. And it's full of frightening photos of dead dolphins with red dolphin blood in the water.

# DAISY'S DOLPHIN NOTES
## DOLPHINS AND HUMANS

The big dangers to dolphins are fishing and pollution.

1. Since the 1950s, millions of Pacific Ocean spinner and spotted dolphins have drowned in fishing nets. Some fishermen trapped dolphins knowing that they were feeding on tuna fish. By catching the dolphins they could be sure of catching the fish.

2. More dolphins die in drift nets. In the northern part of the Pacific Ocean, each night enough nets are set to stretch all the way around the world. And every night, along with fish, they drown hundreds of dolphins and turtles.

HELP I'M TIED UP!

3. Pollution is even more deadly. It includes harmful chemicals made by industry. Poisonous substances such as mercury leak into rivers and seas. The chemicals build up in fish and then inside dolphins when they eat fish, slowly poisoning them.

4. Even if the dolphins survive they're often left weaker and fall victim to germs and

112

> disease. In 1989, tragedy struck Monkey Mia. Several dolphins died suddenly. They may have been poisoned by pollution or died of diseases caused by germs in human sewage.

People care about dolphins – in Europe and America millions of people buy tuna fish that's been caught without harming dolphins. So here's the mystery. Humans love dolphins and we don't want to wipe them out. So why are we doing so much damage to them?

## *September 2*

Today I took a fresh look at the dolphin feeding. Instead of watching the dolphins, I studied the tourists watching them. How do people react to dolphins? That's what I wanted to know.

Well, everyone seems to be affected in a different way and you never can tell what that's going to be. Some people laugh and some people can't stop talking. Before the dolphin feeding, some people, especially youngsters, seem a little afraid. But on the whole, the people are excited.

This morning, Gabby, Splash and Cheeky were lying in the water waiting to be fed. Cheryl was keeping back the tourists, and for a change the volunteer feeders were a boy and his mum. The mum was carrying the heavy fish bucket and the boy was going to feed the dolphins.

The mum was leading her son by the hand and the crowd parted to let them through. The boy seemed unsure and kept looking up at his mum. He looked thin and pale – he was clearly ill. His mum whispered a few words and the boy bit his lip. He looked at the dolphins with big frightened eyes.

The boy's mum helped him to pull a fish out of the bucket. Awkwardly he bent over Splash, who quickly took the fish from his hand. Instantly a look of amazement spread over the boy's face. Without thinking he stretched out his hand and gently touched Splash's side.

Cheryl looked worried. Visitors aren't supposed to touch the dolphins. You can tell if a dolphin doesn't want to be touched, they draw away or even try to bite you. But Splash didn't even move. It was as if she could sense that the boy had a special reason for touching her.

Eventually the boy was led away. All his fears were forgotten and his little face was shining with wonder and excitement. I guessed that touching the dolphin was the most amazing thing he'd ever done. His mum was smiling too, but she also had tears in her eyes. As I said, you never can tell how a dolphin will affect you.

## September 3

I've started to pack. It's my last few days here and although I don't want to go, I know my job with Wildwatch is coming to an end. But before I go home I've got two more days of dolphin watching and I'm determined to make the most of them!

## September 4

Dolphins can drive you crazy! On a day of beautiful clear skies and gentle breezes you set out to watch dolphins, and all you find is a lazy pelican who paddles after your boat and begs for fish scraps.

A LAZY PELICAN

Sam had prawn sandwiches for his lunch. He offered me one, but I've never been a fan of prawns, so I said "no thanks". I nibbled my cheese and pickle sandwiches and tried not to look at the crunchy pink things that Sam was munching.

After lunch we waited for hours, but we didn't spot a single fin. Not one sniff of a dolphin to liven up the long hot afternoon. So instead, Sam told me a story to pass the time...

## The boy and his dolphin

All over the world, some dolphins choose to live close to people. No one knows why they do this, but it happens. This is one of the first stories ever told about such a dolphin.

Nearly 2,000 years ago, a young boy lived beside the blue sea near Naples in Italy. His father was a poor fisherman, but he worked hard and sent his son to school. Every morning the boy had a long walk to school around a narrow bay. And every evening he faced the long weary walk back.

One day the boy stopped to swim in the bay, and he made friends with a dolphin. The dolphin gave the boy a ride across the water. The boy called his dolphin friend Simo, and every morning and evening Simo would come when the boy called him. The two friends would swim in the bay and the dolphin would give the boy a ride across the bay. Thanks to the dolphin the boy no longer had a long walk to and from school.

But one day the boy didn't call for Simo. During the night he had fallen ill and died. It was said the dolphin died too – of a broken heart. But people remembered the story. Hundreds of years later a painting was found on the wall of an ancient Roman house near the bay. The painting was as bright and beautiful as the day it had been painted.

It showed a boy riding on a dolphin's back.

"Why does it have to be so sad?" I asked Sam.

Sam smiled. "That's the way it was," he said gently. "Or maybe it wasn't. Dolphins can't give rides on their backs, it can damage them. The boy probably held on to the dolphin's dorsal fin. But I don't think a dolphin would die of a broken heart."

On the way home I didn't exactly die of a broken heart. But I did feel sad. I felt sad that I only had one more day of dolphin watching. It was my last chance to see Bubble and Squeak. And I knew that I had to see them again – I just had to! Right at the end of the day, Sam let me steer *Cindy* into Monkey Mia. On the last two trips he's let me take the wheel. He says I'm getting good at driving a boat!

### *September 5*

I knew something was wrong when Sam showed up 40 minutes late. There I was stamping crossly up and down the jetty. Where had he got to?

As soon as Sam stuck his head from the cabin window I could see that he wasn't well. He looked pale and tired.

"Are you all right?" I cried.

A look of pain passed over Sam's face. "It must have been those prawns," he moaned. "I've spent the whole night chucking up! I'm not fit…"

"Oh no!" I burst out. I'm sorry to say I wasn't thinking of Sam. I was upset because I would miss seeing the dolphins!

"What are you going to do?" I asked.

"I've got to lie down," Sam groaned. "I don't feel at all well…"

"You'd better come to my caravan," I said grimly.

"But what about you?" Sam asked. "You could take *Cindy* out. It's your last dolphin-watching day."

"Can I?" I said excitedly. "Can I really, Sam? *Yes, please!*"

And so I headed out into the bay on my own. I had no idea where to look for the dolphins. But I hoped they'd hear *Cindy*'s engine and come to me.

And luckily they did!

An hour later, suddenly there they were, looking up at me from the blue water and clicking happily.

It was Bubble and Squeak!

HI-YA, DAISY!

The water sparkled in the warm sunshine and I knew that I had to swim with the dolphins one last time. *Cindy* was floating in shallow water close to a seagrass bank. I heaved the heavy anchor over the side, taking care to miss the dolphins who were playing on the other side of the boat.

The water was deeper than it looked and I got a good mouthful as it closed over my head. I hit the air spluttering and blowing.

"Spbbbbbbbbbb!" A sound close by made me jump. It was Squeak – he'd just blown a raspberry from his blowhole.

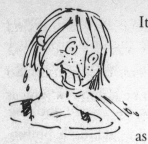

It sounded just like the noise I'd made as I came up a few moments earlier! So I blew a raspberry back at Squeak. "Ssssssbbbbbbbb!" I spluttered as the spit flew from my mouth.

"Spbbbbbbbbbb!" replied Squeak.

My heart gave a leap. The little dolphin was *copying* me! It was almost as if he was talking to me!

"SSSSSSSSSBBBBBBBBB!" I repeated more loudly.

"SPBBBBBBBBBB!" replied Squeak.

And so it was that Daisy Page, a respectable school librarian, spent the next five minutes happily blowing raspberries at a dolphin.

Suddenly Bubble came up close by and without even thinking, I reached out my hands and put them around her dorsal fin. Since dolphins are easily hurt, this is as close as you can get to giving a dolphin a cuddle.

HOLD ON TIGHT!

Bubble didn't try to struggle or shake me off. She just kept moving, at first slowly, and then faster and faster. Suddenly I was gliding.

I looked down and saw the seagrass and white sand passing beneath me. I felt as if I was flying! Floating over an undersea world in a dream of happiness. So this, I thought, is how it feels to be a dolphin. This is how the boy felt in Sam's story…

All at once Bubble rolled and left me floating in the warm quiet sea. We had gone a long way. I could see the boat in the distance, but now she looked like a small dark blob.

And then over to my right I saw something that sent a cold shiver of horror through my body. There in the bright blue water was a dark fin! I'd seen plenty of dolphins in the past two months, but this was no dolphin … it was a shark!

I wanted to escape. Swim for my life – but I knew I'd never make it. The shark would get me first and the faster I tried to swim the faster it would attack. And tiger sharks can kill people.

SLUUURP!

So I stood still on my tiptoes in the water with my heart banging like a steam hammer, thinking. How could I escape? What could I do? The shark was circling, I was sure it was getting closer. The fin cut through the water like a super-sharp knife.

Just my luck, I thought stupidly. The first shark I've seen and I'm in the water with it! I opened my mouth to scream in terror...

And then it happened! Another fin appeared. A grey fin with a white scar circle. It was Bubble and she was heading straight for the shark!

I held my breath. Surely the shark would attack her! But no, the big fierce fish turned away. Now Bubble rolled towards me. I ducked underwater and saw her dark shape. Then she turned and charged the shark once more. And this time she wasn't alone. There were dolphins everywhere – one, two, three, six fins. Gabby, I think, and Splash and Cheeky, Buzz, Smiler and Rags. They'd all come to see off the shark.

But the shark was gone. It knew it was outnumbered and it had decided to leave before the dolphins attacked. With their enemy gone, the dolphins left too. They were swimming fast and buzzing and clicking in high excitement. Numbly I decided it was time for me to move too. And slowly and stiffly I began to swim towards the boat.

"Thank you, Bubble," I said quietly. "Thank you, Squeak. Thank you, dolphins. Thank you so much…"

When I got to Monkey Mia, I told Sam the whole story.

Sam rubbed his eyes and sat up in bed. He was still feeling a bit groggy.

"A shark?" he said. "That's terrible. Are you sure it wasn't just another dolphin?"

"Quite sure."

Sam sighed. "Sounds like you've had a lucky escape!" he said. "It's rare, but it happens. Dolphins can drive off sharks and I guess Bubble was trying to protect her baby."

I nodded. Maybe Sam was right. But deep down I knew Bubble was trying to protect me too…

### Later

I've just been for a walk. After a hot day, it was lovely to feel the cool sand between my toes and the evening breeze in my hair. I gazed out at the bay and the big bright full moon. It looked like a searchlight in the black starry sky.

The breeze blew little waves that danced in the moonlight and vanished in a second. And the moon shone a wide crinkly path that glittered and twinkled on the waves.

Suddenly I heard a splash. Two dolphins rose in the water beyond the jetty. All I could see were their glistening backs arching up and a moment later diving with quick wet flicks of their strong tails. Although it was dark and I was too far away to be sure – I felt certain they were Bubble and Squeak.

So I wished them a silent "goodbye".

## September 6

When I said goodbye to Cheryl she smiled and gave me a hug.

"I'm certainly going to miss you," Cheryl said. "For one thing, it's going to be a lot quieter round here!"

"I'm going to miss you too, Cheryl," I laughed. "And everyone here. The whole place in fact!"

"Well," said Cheryl, "you don't have to go. I've heard there's a job coming up at Shark Bay School. They're looking for someone to run their library."

I smiled and shook my head. After the last two months, working in a library seemed a world away. A whole lifetime away.

I said goodbye to Sam this morning. After a better night's rest on his boat, he was feeling a lot stronger. He was almost back to his old self.

"Well, I guess it's goodbye," he said. "The boat's going to feel empty without you."

"I'm going to miss you, Sam," I said. And I knew I would. He looked so noble in the golden morning light with the dawn wind ruffling his hair.

Sam gave me a thoughtful look. "Well, you can come back any time you like," he offered. "I could always use some help and the dolphins would love to see you!"

"Yes, I know they would!" I cried, and plonked a big kiss on his scratchy stubbly cheek.

# DAISY'S DECISION

## *October 10*

On the day I was due to leave, I went for a final early-morning walk. As the sun rose, the clouds blushed a soft seashell pink and the whole bay turned golden and shiny.

DAWN AT MONKEY MIA

As I strolled along the beach I kicked my shoes in the clean white sand. And all the time I was thinking, thinking, thinking. And as I was thinking I was gazing at the bay. The only sound was the lapping of the gentle waves. Above me a few gulls swooped and circled, their wings shining golden in the morning light. It was so beautiful that I wanted to cry. I wanted to cry because I had to go.

All my plans were made. Eric was coming to pick me up from the Overlander Roadhouse at ten. And yet, and yet…

From deep inside my heart, a silent voice shouted "But I don't want to go!"

I don't want to go, I thought.

"You don't *have* to go," said the voice inside me.

"I don't have to go!" I said aloud.

"Do what your heart tells you," said the silent voice. "You want to stay – you *know* you do."

"I want to stay!" I said aloud.

And as soon as I'd said those words I began to laugh and clap my hands.

And that's how I made my decision.

I'm finishing my diary now. But it's not really the end, just a new beginning. I got the job at Shark Bay School. I've started sorting out their books – there's lots of dolphin books and I'm going to buy even more! I expect I'll buy this diary when it's made into a book! And of course, I'll get to read the dolphin books first. That's one of the perks of being a librarian!

But best of all are my days off with Sam in the boat. At this time of year the days are always burning hot and we have to start before dawn. As the sun rises from the shining sea and the bright blue sky warms with summer heat, I gaze about me for the distant flash of a grey fin. And I look forward to another perfect day of diving with dolphins...